WITH SPECIAL THANKS TO LINDA CHAPMAN

First published in Great Britain in 2012 by Simon and Schuster UK Ltd
A CBS COMPANY

Text Copyright © Hothouse Fiction Limited 2012
Illustrations copyright © Mary Hall 2012
Designed by Amy Cooper

The right of Mary Hall to be identified as the illustrator of this work has been asserted by her
in accordance with sections 77 and 78 of the Copyright, Designs and Patents Act, 1988.

1 3 5 7 9 10 8 6 4 2

Simon & Schuster UK Ltd
1st Floor, 222 Gray's Inn Road
London
WC1X 8HB

Simon & Schuster Australia, Sydney

Simon & Schuster India, New Delhi

A CIP catalogue record for this book is available from the British Library.

ISBN 978-0-85707-248-1

This book is a work of fiction. Names, characters, places and incidents are either the product
of the author's imagination or are used fictitiously. Any resemblance to actual people living or
dead, events or locales is entirely coincidental.

Printed and bound by CPI Group (UK) Ltd, Croydon, CR0 4YY
www.simonandschuster.co.uk
www.simonandschuster.com.au
www.spellsisters.co.uk

AMBER CASTLE

LILY
THE FOREST SISTER

Illustrations by Mary Hall

SIMON & SCHUSTER

Silver Hill

Croxton Manor

Morgana's Lair

Avalon

St. Stephen's Church

Fairview Vineyard

Woolston Manor

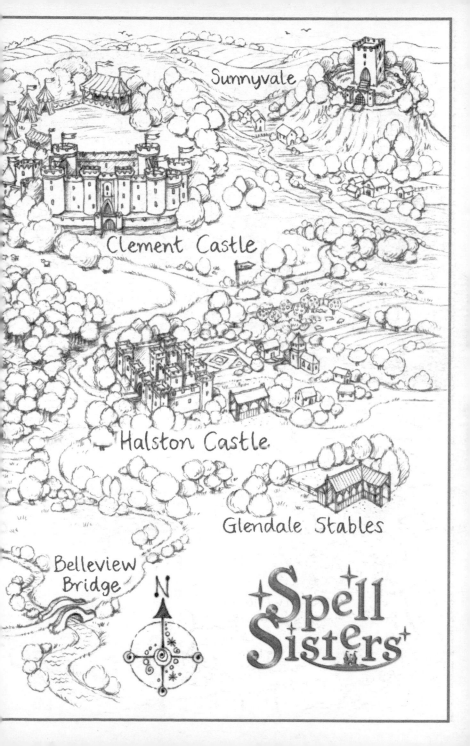

Sunnyvale

Clement Castle

Halston Castle

Glendale Stables

Belleview Bridge

N

Spell Sisters

In a Forest Clearing

Astrangely beautiful woman stood in the middle of a clearing in front of a hollowed-out oak tree. Her long hair was as black as the feathers of the raven that was perched on her shoulder and her jet eyes glittered in her pale face. All around her, the forest was decorated with the russets and yellows of autumn.

Lifting one hand, Morgana Le Fay pointed

at the horse chestnut trees in front of her. Instantly the red and gold leaves started to turn brown and wither. One by one they dropped from the trees to the ground, leaving the branches bare. Morgana smiled cruelly and then clenched her fist, whispering a sinister-sounding spell. The trees' bark slowly blackened, their branches creaking in protest as they twisted into unnatural shapes.

The raven cackled in delight and Morgana laughed with him as she watched the devastation she had caused with her magic.

'The power over all living plants is mine to use as I will,' she hissed. 'It is magic I have taken from Lily, Spell Sister of Avalon. Seven of the eight sisters still remain in their prisons, trapped by my magic. Soon the island of Avalon shall become mine, and mine alone. Those wretched mortal girls may have freed one of my sisters and taken away my control over fire, but they will not beat me again.'

The raven cawed in agreement.

Morgana stroked his feathers. 'The spell cast by Nineve, the Lady of the Lake, is keeping me from claiming Avalon, but that will only last until the next lunar eclipse. After that, nothing will be able to stop me, as long as the Spell Sisters remain trapped. And they shall!' Her cold laugh rang out. 'I will make absolutely sure of it. Nothing and no one shall stop me!' She clapped her hands and then she and the raven vanished, leaving only the blackened trees and undergrowth behind. . .

1

In The Castle

Gwen edged closer to the crackling fire in the enormous fireplace in the Great Hall of her uncle's castle and stretched out her hands towards the flames. The warmth was very welcome. Now that it was autumn, the air always felt slightly damp and cold, even indoors. Nearby, on the window seat in the parlour, her Aunt Matilda was talking to Gwen's cousin, Flora.

'I am very pleased with your attitude towards your studies, Flora. I have a reward for you. I am going to give you this headband, which belonged to my own mother, your grandmother.'

Gwen fidgeted with her dress as her aunt showed Flora a delicate gold band, studded with pearls.

Flora's pretty face lit up. 'Oh, thank you, Mother!'

Aunt Matilda smiled. 'Why don't you try it on?' She carefully fixed the hairband in place on Flora's head, rearranging Flora's two long blonde braids that were trimmed with red cord.

Gwen felt happy for her cousin. The two girls were best friends, and Gwen knew how much Flora liked to please her mother. Gwen certainly wasn't jealous about Flora's new gift. She didn't care for things like that. Her deep red hair hung loose on her shoulders. If Gwen had been given a present she'd have wanted a new bow or a quiver full of arrows!

'It looks very elegant, Flora,' Aunt Matilda said, smoothing down a few stray strands of her daughter's hair. 'You will be careful with it though, won't you, my dear?'

'Of course, Mother,' Flora replied.

'Maybe you should take it off before you go outside,' Aunt Matilda went on, looking worried. 'We all know you can be a little clumsy at times.'

'I won't lose it, Mother. I'll be careful,' Flora said. 'I promise.'

'Very well. Now, you know what you're supposed to be doing this morning?'

Flora nodded. 'Gwen and I are to go and gather some fresh herbs to spread around the upstairs chambers.'

Her mother nodded. 'That's right. And no stopping to play with the pages on the way.' She looked over and fixed Gwen with a warning look. 'Do you understand, Guinevere?'

Gwen hastily pulled herself to attention. 'Yes, Aunt Matilda,' she murmured, giving a little curtsey. She was trying her best to be lady-like, but inside her heart sank. Her aunt was so strict! She only ever wanted Gwen and Flora to do things that she considered suitable for young ladies, which meant learning all the boring duties involved with managing a large household. Gwen found it so frustrating. She longed to be like the pages and be able to learn exciting things like how to fight properly with a sword and a lance. That would be much more fun!

'Now, Guinevere can you tell me which

herbs you will pick?'

Gwen didn't have any idea. 'Um. . . well. . .'

'Come on, child,' Aunt Matilda said impatiently. 'A noble lady should know this. Which herbs will be best at this time of year?'

Flora rescued Gwen. 'Tansy, thyme and rosemary, Mother,' she said quickly. 'Rosemary for health, thyme for its sweet scent and tansy because it brings good fortune.'

Her mother gave her an approving smile. 'Correct, Flora. Guinevere, you would do well to learn from your cousin and spend less time with a bow and arrow in your hands. Your parents sent you here to learn how to perform the duties expected of a young noblewoman, not how to run around outdoors with the boys. I think you sometimes forget that.'

'Yes, Aunt Matilda,' Gwen said meekly,

although inside she was already itching with impatience to be out and away. She was glad her parents had decided to send her to live with Aunt Matilda and Uncle Richard at Halston Castle because it meant she had Flora for company, but her aunt had so many rules it was hard to always be well behaved.

'Off you go then,' Aunt Matilda told them.

As soon as the big wooden door was shut behind them and they were on the staircase, Gwen grabbed Flora's arm. 'Quick come on, let's get going!'

Flora turned to Gwen in surprise. 'You never want to go to the herb garden, Gwen! Why are you so keen?'

Gwen grinned. 'Ah, but you see I happen to know that Evans, the fletcher who makes arrows for the king, delivered some new arrows

to Uncle Richard this morning, and they're in the upstairs chambers.'

'So?' Flora frowned.

'So, I really want to see them!' Gwen replied. 'Evans's arrows have flights made from swan feathers, peacock feathers. . . even kingfisher feathers! And he carves the metal point of the arrows into the most wonderful patterns too! So the faster we gather the herbs, the quicker we'll get to the chambers so I can catch a glimpse of the arrows!'

Flora shook her head and laughed. 'I should have known it would be something to do with archery. Oh well, I don't mind. I like gathering herbs.'

'You like everything to do with running a household. You're going to be such a good lady of the manor when you're older,' Gwen teased her.

'And what's wrong with that?' protested Flora. 'I think it's really interesting learning about household things.'

Gwen pulled a face. 'Learning how to store fruit, and what food to eat, and what things bring good luck, and what herbs to use? How can you say that's interesting, Flora? Riding, shooting, being out in the forest – they're interesting things ... exciting things!' She sighed and pushed a hand through her tangle of red hair. 'Oh, I wish we could have another adventure!'

Flora's eyes caught hers. 'Well, maybe we will soon.' They shared a secret smile.

A week ago, the two girls had the most amazing adventure together. It had all started when they had decided to visit the beautiful Lake hidden in the forest near the castle. In the centre of the Lake was a mysterious island called Avalon that was always shrouded in a purple mist. On the day they had gone there, Flora and Gwen had found a silver necklace with a blue pendant caught in a rock by the water's edge. Flora hadn't been able to pull it free, but Gwen had, and when she'd released it from the rock, it had magically floated into the air and fastened round her neck!

Gwen looked down at the pendant, which was still round her neck, hanging on a silver chain.

'I don't think anything more magical has ever happened to me than when I pulled the necklace out of the rock!'

Flora nodded, her eyes shining with the memory. 'I know! And then Nineve appeared...'

Nineve, the beautiful Lady of the Lake, had risen up through the water and told the girls that the magical island of Avalon was in dreadful trouble. An evil sorceress called Morgana Le Fay had captured the eight Spell Sisters who lived there. Morgana had imprisoned each of them in a different way and taken their powers for herself and left the island dying without its magic. Now Morgana was determined to reach the island itself, claim it for her own and keep the magic she had stolen. Nineve had explained to the girls that she'd tried to prevent the sorceress by casting a spell that stopped Morgana from crossing the Lake, but the spell was weakening with each passing day and, come the next lunar eclipse, Morgana would be able to reach the island. An ancient prophecy had foreseen that a mortal girl who could pull the necklace out of the rock would be able to free the eight Spell Sisters of Avalon and save the magical island, for its future was entwined with the fortunes of the kingdom itself. Gwen was that girl! She had immediately offered to help – Flora too.

On that first day, they had freed Sophia, the sister who's magic controlled fire. Sophia had given Gwen a fire agate stone to add to her necklace as a gift when she had returned to Avalon, saying that Gwen might need it one day. Gwen touched the gemstone now, remembering how Avalon had started to come back to life once the released sister had set foot on the island.

'I hope Nineve can locate the other sisters for us to go and rescue soon,' Gwen said, looking anxiously at Flora. 'Without them, Avalon's magic is going to fade to nothing. Who knows what will happen then?'

Nineve had told the girls she would try and track the other Spell Sisters down, and then she would use the pendant to let Gwen and Flora know each time she found one of them. *But when*

will that be? Gwen thought longingly.

She and Flora went to their bedchamber and began to get ready to go outside. They put on their thick outdoor cloaks and boots and, while Flora fussed with her new headband, and tied then retied the bows at the ends of her two long braids, Gwen simply slung her bow over her shoulder, hung her quiver of arrows around her waist and picked up her leather travelling bag.

'Come along!' Gwen said to her cousin with a smile. 'We're only going to gather herbs!'

But Flora was still checking her outfit, and then she picked up her bottle of perfume oil and dabbed a little on her neck.

'What are you doing that for?' Gwen gave her a

sly look. 'Are you hoping to meet the pages?'

'No!' Flora said, blushing and slipping the bottle into her pocket.

'Which one do you like then?' Gwen grinned.

'None of them! I just like to wear perfume!' Flora tossed her head and marched to the door. But her elegant exit was ruined by her tripping over a pair of Gwen's shoes. 'Whoa!' she exclaimed as she stumbled forward.

Gwen caught her just before she fell over.

'Thanks,' Flora sighed. 'Oh, why am I always so clumsy?'

'You're not that clumsy – well, only a little bit,' said Gwen. 'Anyway, it could be useful. If you tripped over near the pages maybe one of them would catch you!' She pretended to be Flora and dramatically clutched a hand to her forehead.

'Oh, Will! Catch me please!'

Flora hit her arm but giggled.

'Come on,' said Gwen with a laugh.

They went downstairs and hurried across the grassy castle keep talking and laughing. The cold autumn air was sharp as a knife blade, and Gwen could smell the tangy wood smoke wafting up the hill from the villagers' cottages. She breathed in deeply. Inside the castle she always felt confined, but outside she felt happy and free.

She and Flora went over the drawbridge and down the hill, past the stone armoury and the barns where the hay and straw were kept, past the kennels where the hunting dogs were barking, and past the archery butts where Gwen and the pages practised shooting at round archery targets.

Gwen touched her bow, wishing she could stop there. Archery was one of her favourite things in the world – she loved the smooth elm wood of her bow and the feeling of letting loose an arrow, watching it fly swiftly away from her and hit a target dead centre.

'Oh, no you don't,' said Flora, reading Gwen's thoughts as she started to slow down. 'We've got to keep going. Mother will be cross if we take too long and, like you said, the quicker we gather the herbs the sooner you can try and see Father's arrows.'

Gwen sighed, but knew Flora was right.

They made their way out of the courtyard and over past the church and the small stone house that belonged to Thomas the priest.

'At least the orchard's close,' said Gwen. The walled orchard and herb garden was just behind Thomas's house, across some common land where pigs were tethered. The trees in the orchard were heavy with fruit, the sweet scent of the ripe apples and pears filling the air.

The two girls started to fill the basket with tansy, rosemary and thyme.

They had just finished when Flora swooped down on something lying among the plants. 'Look! I think it's from a dove!' she said, holding up a pure white feather.

Gwen frowned. 'Is that good luck or bad?' She knew there were many rules in the castle about the things that were supposed to bring different fortunes.

'Good, of course!' Flora told her. She chanted a rhyme:

'The white feather brings fortune good and true
While iron fights evil through and through.
Ravens and bats should be kept from the room
Or bad luck will come, bringing death and doom.'

Flora twirled the feather in her hands. 'I'm going to put this in our chamber and see if it brings us good luck. Mother told me she found a white feather once and the very next day, she found

her favourite hair comb that she'd lost. Not only that, but when she slept with the feather under her pillow, the next morning, her backache had completely gone.'

'But how can a feather make that happen?' said Gwen disbelievingly.

'I don't know, but it does,' Flora insisted. 'Feathers are really magical – kingfisher feathers are as good as horseshoes at warding off evil spirits and—' Flora broke off as they heard the sound of boys' voices just outside the orchard.

'It's the pages!' Gwen exclaimed. She shot a teasing look at Flora. 'Do you want to put some more perfume on before we say hello?'

Darting away to avoid Flora's playful punch, Gwen ran to the orchard entrance.

'Come on, let's go!'

Teaching A Lesson

There were six pages who lived at the castle. The youngest, Tom, was eight, and the oldest, Will, was just fourteen. It was normal for noble families to send their sons away to live with another noble family and learn the things they needed to in order to become a knight. Just like the girls were sent away to learn how to perform the duties that would be expected of them when they were older and became lady of the manor.

'Faster! Faster!' Tom was getting a piggyback ride from thirteen-year-old Arthur, Gwen's favourite page. Tom's legs kicked and he beat Arthur around the head.

Arthur stopped dead and dumped the boy on the ground.

'Ow!' Tom complained. 'What did you do that for?'

'That's how a horse will treat you if you beat him like that,' Arthur told him.

'Saint Arthur, always looking out for the animals,' said Will, the oldest page, who never lost any chance to put Arthur down.

Tom jumped to his feet, not at all upset. 'Sorry, Arthur! Can I have another go?'

But Arthur had spotted Gwen and Flora. He waved and headed over to them.

'Hello,' Gwen said, smiling at him.

'I like your necklace, Gwen,' Arthur said, his eyes catching on her pendant and the fire agate stone. 'Where's it from?'

Gwen looked down. 'Oh . . . I just, um, found it. . .'

'What do you think of my new headband, Arthur?' Flora interjected, attempting to distract him from the necklace. 'Mother just gave it to me for doing well at my studies!'

Arthur smiled. 'Very nice.' But his eyes looked back at Gwen's necklace. 'Where did you find it?'

Gwen was saved from answering by Will coming over. 'So what are you two doing?' he said to her and Flora. 'Oh,' he sneered slightly as he took in their basket filled with herbs. 'I might have guessed. You're doing girls' work.' He gave

Gwen a look. 'Well, it's good to see you doing things that girls should do, instead of trying to copy us boys. You need to do what's expected of you and keep to your place.'

Gwen felt hot anger rise inside her. She was loads better than Will at archery, and she could climb and run as well as most of the boys too. He knew that! How dare he say she should only do things that were expected of her! She put her hands on her hips and was about to make a sharp retort when she caught sight of Black Spot, one of the pigs, rooting around on the ground just behind them. He was tethered with a long rope and had churned the ground around him into a mess of mud and pig muck. An idea popped into her head and she bit back a smile.

'Oh, I should stick to my place, should I? Well, I'm as good as you at plenty of things,' she said to him. 'Why don't we see how well you do at a challenge?'

'I. . . I haven't got my bow, so we can't have an archery contest,' Will said quickly.

Coward! Gwen thought, knowing full well that even if he had his bow he wouldn't take her on at an archery contest because he knew she would beat him.

'Hmmm. . .' She pretended to think. 'Well, how about we see who can run fastest?'

'I'll easily beat you at running,' Will said with a scornful smirk.

Gwen gritted her teeth. 'Well, if it's going to be that easy, then why don't we make it harder and by having a running backwards race? We'll see who can go the furthest without falling over. We can start here, and the one to stumble soonest loses.'

'That's a stupid challenge!' sneered Will.

'Are you scared you might be beaten by a girl?' Gwen said slyly.

A few of the other pages grinned and started making clucking noises. Will flushed. 'Of course I'm not! Challenge accepted!'

'All right then,' Gwen said, manoeuvring herself round so Will would be running backwards towards where Black Spot was rooting round in the grass and mud. 'On my mark. . .'

Will hesitated, suddenly seeming to sense she might be up to something. 'Why do you get to decide everything? I'll say when we start.'

Gwen shrugged and positioned herself next

to Will, making sure he would be in the path of the rooting pig. Will puffed out his chest. 'OK then! Ready . . . go!'

The other pages whooped as Will and Gwen started to run backwards – all apart from Arthur, who had seen exactly what Gwen was planning and was watching agog. Gwen ran backwards steadily, glancing to the side to see if Will was still heading in the right direction. Would her plan work?

Will was pulling ahead of her in the race, and grinned smugly as Gwen stumbled a little, but kept her footing.

'Oh dear, watch your step, you wouldn't want to get your lovely dress dirty!' he puffed mockingly, but Gwen just smiled. She could see what was about to happen as she glanced over her shoulder. . .

Thwack!

Will ran straight into Black Spot, who gave a startled grunt. 'Wahhhh!' Will yelled, his arms flailing as he tried to keep his balance on the slippery mud. Black Spot gave an angry snort and charged forwards, butting him in the back. Will tumbled over and landed with a splat right in a pile of pig muck. Gwen slowed to a stop and put her hands on her hips.

'Yuck!' Will shouted. Black Spot came back over to him, snorting and snuffling at his face with his hairy snout. 'Get off me, you great dirty pig!' howled Will, batting him away with his arms and covering himself in even more muck.

All the other pages fell about laughing.

Gwen's eyes sparkled. 'It's good to see you keeping to your place, Will – with the pigs!' She reached down and offered him a hand up, but

he shook his head and folded his arms huffily. The other pages hooted and clutched their sides as Gwen shrugged and strode away.

Flora ran after her. 'Gwen!' she hissed. 'You knew Will was going to run into Black Spot! You shouldn't have done something like that.'

Gwen looked at her. 'Why not? He shouldn't be so mean. Boys are no better than girls and he should know it.'

'But the boys always are mean and they tease us. I suppose we just have to accept it, don't we?' Flora sighed.

Gwen raised her eyebrows. 'Not me – and you shouldn't either, Flora. Anyway, we don't need them.' She linked arms with her cousin and smiled. 'We can have fun on our own, can't we!'

Flora nodded and looked at Gwen with reluctant admiration. 'You're right about that!'

Gwen grinned. 'Good. Now, let's go and see those new arrows back in the castle!'

3

A Magical Message

Gwen's heart thudded with excitement as she ran up the winding stairs to Uncle Richard and Aunt Matilda's private chamber on the third floor of the castle. It held their sleeping quarters and a large room where Uncle Richard conducted his business as lord of the manor. Gwen and Flora didn't often get to go in there. Gwen wondered if the arrows would be somewhere obvious? What would they look like?

She turned the big black metal handle and pushed the door open. 'Hurry up, Flora!' she urged impatiently. 'I—'

She broke off as she saw the tall, dark-haired figure of her uncle standing inside in front of the fire. 'Oh, Uncle Richard! Sorry, I wasn't expecting you to be in here!'

Gwen hesitated in the doorway. Her uncle was a man of varying moods. When he lost his temper he was scary, but at the moment he seemed to be in good humour. He smiled at her. 'Come in, child,' he boomed.

Flora arrived just behind Gwen.

'Ah, and my daughter too,' he said, his smile widening. 'What brings you girls here?'

'We've brought some herbs for your room,

Father,' Flora replied meekly, showing him the basket.

'Excellent! I was only saying to your mother this morning that we could do with some more. Go ahead and spread them over the floor.'

Flora began to scatter the herbs through the rushes that covered the stone floor. The sweet fragrance of the tansy, thyme and rosemary started filling the air, chasing away the stuffy smell of the tallow candles that dripped wax over the iron candleholders in the wall. Gwen helped Flora, but she couldn't help feeling bitterly disappointed. Now she wouldn't be able to see the arrows after all!

Uncle Richard headed over to his dark wooden desk and sat down behind it, picking up a goblet of wine. He took a mouthful and spluttered. 'Goodness! This wine from the new vineyard is awfully sour!'

'Shall I go to the kitchen and get you some different wine, Father?' Flora offered immediately.

'No, no. You girls have a job to do with those herbs. It will do me no harm to walk to the kitchen and back.' Uncle Richard strode to the door and disappeared down the staircase with his goblet.

As soon as he had gone, Gwen dashed over to a table at the side of the room where she had spotted the new arrows laid out. 'Oh, Flora! Look at these!' she breathed.

The shafts were smooth and polished, the nocks where the arrows fitted made of ivory, and the flights from all different feathers. Gwen spotted peacock feathers, swan feathers, kingfisher feathers. She picked one of the arrows with a kingfisher flight, admiring the unusual

blue-and-green feathers tied on with golden thread, the engraved pointed iron tip, the carving on it so wonderfully detailed. Her own arrows were made of simple wood with plain arrowheads and hen feathers for flights. Her fingers itched to have her bow and try and shoot an arrow like this.

'Well, look who I met on the stairs.' Her uncle's voice rang out as he reappeared in the doorway. Gwen jumped guiltily, hastily hiding the kingfisher arrow behind her back.

Her uncle came into the room with Thomas the priest.

'We have business to discuss this afternoon. Have you finished, girls?'

'Yes, Father,' said Flora, putting the last stalks of thyme down on the floor. 'We're done now.'

'I didn't make it down to the kitchen – will you find your mother and ask her to fetch me some new wine?'

'Of course, Father.' Flora went to the door and looked at Gwen. Gwen hesitated, not knowing what to do – she still had the kingfisher arrow hidden behind her back! She saw her uncle looking at her with his beetle-black eyes under his shaggy eyebrows. She couldn't put it back in front of him – he'd be so cross that she was touching his new arrows... *I'll sneak back later and put it back then,* she thought.

Keeping it hidden behind her back, she quickly joined Flora at the door. Her uncle wasn't paying the girls any attention – he was already talking to Thomas the priest in his booming voice. 'Well, well, Thomas, we have much to discuss...'

The girls slipped out of the door. 'Flora, I'm going to have to go back later on,' Gwen whispered. She showed Flora the arrow.

'Gwen! Father will be furious if he knows you have one of his new arrows.'

'I know. I didn't mean to take it,' Gwen said quickly. 'I was just looking at it when he came back in. I'll return it as soon as I can...' She broke off as she felt a strange tingling feeling around her neck. She looked down at the same moment as Flora gasped.

'Your pendant, Gwen! It's glowing!'

In the dim light of the staircase, the blue stone around Gwen's neck was casting out a silvery, sparkly light. Gwen picked the pendant up and almost dropped it again as a mist seemed to swirl inside it and then the face of a beautiful young woman appeared. She had long chestnut hair held back by a sparkling pearl headband. 'Nineve!' Gwen breathed.

'Gwen,' the Lady of the Lake answered, her voice whispering out from the pendant. 'I need your help again. I have found the next Spell Sister. Come to the Lake so that I can use my magic to show you where she is hidden.'

'When?' whispered Gwen.

'As soon as you can. There is no time to waste.'

Gwen looked up at her cousin. 'Flora, we should go now.'

'We can't just go sneaking off to the forest,' Flora protested. 'People will wonder where we are.'

'Not until supper time,' Gwen argued. 'No one's going to miss us this afternoon. We can tell your mother about Uncle's wine and then go. We've done all our chores for today.'

She saw Flora hesitate.

'We have to do this, Flora!' Gwen insisted. 'Nineve and the Spell Sisters need us!'

Flora lifted her chin. 'You're right. We can't let them down!'

Gwen held up the pendant. 'We're coming, Nineve!' she said in excitement. 'We'll leave straight away!'

'Travel swiftly,' Nineve urged, and then a mist passed across the pendant again, clearing her image. . .

The Second Spell Sister

Gwen and Flora quickly found Aunt Matilda in the kitchen. She was talking to Hal, the castle's cook. The girls told her about Uncle Richard's wine.

'That's the second bad barrel we've had from the Fairview vineyard this week,' Aunt Matilda tutted to Hal. 'We only opened the new barrel a few days ago, how can it be sour already?' She looked at Flora and Gwen, who were already heading towards the door. 'Now where are you two going?'

'Just out,' said Gwen. 'For a walk in the gardens. To talk, and maybe gather some flowers,' she added.

Her aunt nodded approvingly. 'That sounds entirely appropriate. And remember girls, be lady-like.'

Forgetting her aunt's words as soon as they were out of the kitchen, Gwen raced out of the castle, over the drawbridge and down the hill towards the woods, with Flora following swiftly behind.

Gwen often went into the forest to climb and explore and practise her archery, but Flora usually avoided them. As they set off along the path, Gwen ran ahead, not caring about the mud and brambles, but Flora picked her way gingerly through the puddles trying not to fall over or get too dirty.

As they got further away from the castle and deeper into the trees she shivered. 'There's still a really strange feeling in the air. Do you feel it too?'

Gwen nodded. The week before, they had both noticed that the air around the Lake had seemed very quiet and that the plants and trees were starting to die. They weren't as near to the Lake yet but, looking around, Gwen saw that many of the plants seemed to be suffering here as well. Instead of the leaves hanging golden and red on the branches as they were nearer the castle, they were brown and dull, many of them lying on the ground, others caught in big clumps on the branches. The rosehips had withered on the bushes and the blackberries, usually so plump and juicy in the autumn, were nearly all shrivelled up.

'I bet it's because of Avalon's magic fading,' Gwen said uneasily. 'The effects must be starting to spread out beyond the Lake and further into the forest. Oh, Flora, we have to rescue all the sisters and stop Morgana Le Fay. Imagine if the whole kingdom ends up like this!'

Flora looked alarmed. 'We mustn't let that happen!'

They began to run, pushing brambles aside, Flora stumbling and tripping over tree roots until Gwen grabbed her hand to help her along. Panting for breath, they eventually burst through the trees. The Lake's glasslike waters were covered with a swirling purple mist. Gwen knew that in the centre of the mist was the island of Avalon.

'Nineve!' she called softly. 'We're here!' To her delight, a silver light shone out over a spot on the Lake.

'Look!' cried Flora.

The light grew brighter and brighter, and started to move towards them. As it did so, the waters parted and the Lady of the Lake rose up from the depths in her blue-and-green gown. Her chestnut hair fell all the way to her bare feet.

'Gwen! Flora!' She held out her arms and ran lightly across the surface of the water towards them. She stopped at the water's edge, not stepping out on to the land. Gwen knew that if Nineve left the Lake, the magic spell she had cast to keep Morgana from crossing the water would weaken. Nineve had to stay in the Lake now until all eight Spell Sisters were back on the island.

Gwen kicked off her leather boots and

waded in a little way. The water was icy cold against her toes and ankles but she didn't care. Nineve hugged her. 'Thank you for coming so quickly, girls.'

'Of course! We want to help so much. Which sister have you found? Where do we have to go? Where is she trapped?' The questions tumbled out of Gwen.

Nineve's beautiful face looked worried. 'Using my magic, I have found where Lily, the sister whose magic controls plants, is trapped. I cannot tell you exactly where she is or how she is being imprisoned – you must find that out for yourselves – but I can show you all that my magic has revealed to me. Watch. . .'

Gwen stepped out of the water and she and Flora gazed from the rocks at the Lakeside as Nineve cupped her hands together. Shutting her eyes, the Lady of the Lake whispered a few words and then slowly opened her hands. A white mist appeared between her palms and then floated away. As it cleared, it revealed a pure white water lily.

Gwen and Flora caught their breath.

'It's beautiful,' Flora said in an awed voice.

Very gently, Nineve set the water lily down on the still surface of the Lake. She blew softly and the lily floated towards Gwen and Flora. As it passed over the water, the Lake seemed to shimmer silver and an image formed.

'Watch,' Nineve said again softly.

Gwen leaned forward, her heart beating fast. What were they going to see?

In the Lake, a picture of a vineyard formed with a stone farmhouse and a couple of outbuildings. The farmhouse was deserted, the grass was long around it and the vines were overgrown and dying, with stunted bunches of rotting black grapes hanging low on the branches. Around the vineyard was a high, forbidding wall. The entrance was through a massive gate, its black metal twisted into strange patterns and covered with overgrown vine tendrils and leaves.

'I know that vineyard!' exclaimed Gwen. 'I remember coming past it when I first came to live at the castle. It's Fairview – the place where Aunt Matilda said they got the barrels of wine that had spoiled. It's on the other side of the forest.'

'It looks horrible. No wonder Father said the wine tasted sour. Why are all the vines are dying?' Flora asked Nineve.

'Because of Morgana. Now she has Lily's magic she has power over plants and she is making the land suffer, and her evil is spreading fast. You must free Lily. Once she has been released, her magical ability to control plants will return to her and the plants Morgana has enchanted will recover.'

Gwen felt a wave of determination rush through her. 'We'll do it!'

Flora nodded and took Gwen's hand.

'Do you remember what you need to do to free the sisters when you find them?' Nineve asked them quickly.

'Yes,' Gwen answered. She felt as if it was engraved on her memory. 'I have to hold the pendant to wherever they're trapped and say: Spell Sister of Avalon I now release; Return to the island and help bring peace.'

A smile caught at Nineve's mouth. 'Well done. When you get to the vineyard, remember that Lily will probably be disguised or transformed by Morgana's magic, just as Sophia was. You must look very carefully for her. She could be anywhere.'

The girls both nodded.

'It's going to take us a while to walk to the vineyard,' said Flora anxiously.

'Who's planning on walking?' Gwen said,

with a twinkle in her eye. 'I think someone's been following us. . .' She turned to the trees and let out a piercing whistle.

'Moonlight!' cried Flora as a beautiful, snow-white stallion burst out of the trees and galloped straight over to them with a whinny. 'He remembers us!'

'Of course he does,' said Gwen, stroking the stallion's warm neck. He rubbed his head against her. 'I bet you've been wanting to have another adventure too, haven't you, boy?'

The stallion neighed softly and tossed his head as if he was nodding. Gwen hugged him. When she and Flora had set off to rescue the first sister, Sophia, they had found the wild horse in the forest. Gwen had made friends with him and then fed him with an apple that had come from Avalon. From the moment he had eaten it, it had given him magical powers. He was able to understand them, and he could gallop far more swiftly than any normal horse. When they had returned to the castle, they had decided to leave him in the forest rather than risk taking him to the stables where he would have become one of her uncle's horses, but Gwen had been longing to see him again.

Flora patted him too. 'It's so lovely to see you, Moonlight!' He snorted happily, his dark eyes shining, his coat like freshly fallen snow.

Taking hold of his silky mane, Gwen vaulted easily on to his back, pulling her long skirts up and out of the way.

'Definitely not lady-like, Gwen,' said Flora with a grin. 'Mother would not approve.'

Gwen chuckled. 'Oh, dear. What are you going to do?'

'Get up too, of course!' said Flora, laughing. Gwen put out her hand and helped her cousin scramble up behind her.

They both turned to look down at Nineve, who was still standing on the surface of the water. 'We'll find Lily and bring her back!' Gwen said. 'We won't let you down.'

'May Avalon speed you on your way!' the Lady of the Lake declared.

Moonlight whinnied and then wheeled round and galloped off. As they reached the trees, Gwen looked over her shoulder and saw Nineve's beautiful face creased in an anxious frown, as she sank slowly back into the Lake.

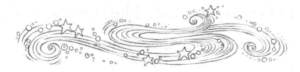

5

Hide and Seek

Gwen felt excitement racing through her as the world swept by. Moonlight swerved around the tree trunks, leaped over muddy puddles and whizzed down the narrow forest paths. His long mane swept around the two girls. It was wonderful to ride him again. But would they manage to rescue Lily? It might not just be as simple as finding the trapped sister and freeing her. Gwen thought back to when she and Flora had freed Sophia. Morgana had realised what they were doing and sent a flock of vicious birds to stop them. There was every chance she would try and stop them this time too. . .

Gwen was jolted from her thoughts when she heard Flora give a sudden shriek. 'Oh no! My headband's fallen off! We've got to stop and get it!'

Gwen glanced over her shoulder. 'We can't.'

'Please,' Flora begged. 'Mother will be so cross if I lose it. I promised her I would be careful with it, and if we come back without it she'll know we've been doing something we shouldn't.'

Gwen saw the worry in her cousin's face. She was right – Aunt Matilda would probably ask all sorts of questions as to where it had got lost and keep a closer eye on both of them from now on. They couldn't afford risking their mission to rescue the other sisters by making her aunt suspicious. 'All right.' Gwen pulled on Moonlight's mane. 'Whoa, boy!'

Moonlight gave a surprised snort and slowed to a trot. He came to a halt. Gwen patted his neck and slipped off his back. 'We'll be as quick as we can.'

Flora dismounted too. Moonlight pawed away at the fallen leaves and put his head down to graze on some grass at the side of the track. The girls quickly started to walk back the way they had come. 'I think it might have fallen off around here, but I'm not sure,' said Flora. She started hunting through the undergrowth and fallen leaves.

'Well, why don't you look here and I'll go back a bit further in case it fell off earlier?'

suggested Gwen. She could feel frustration gnawing inside her like a dog with a bone. She wanted to get to the vineyard and start looking for Lily, but she knew Flora hated getting into trouble, and Aunt Matilda would be really cross if Flora went back to the castle without her new headband. Hopefully it will turn up quickly, Gwen thought.

She hurried through the trees, her sharp eyes sweeping over the muddy puddles and the brambles, looking for a telltale shine of metal. She caught a glint of something among some bushes and eagerly swooped down – but it was just an old horseshoe lost by a traveller who must have passed by this way. She picked it up and slipped it into her bag. Horseshoes brought good luck because they were made of iron, which could supposedly scare evil spirits away. We're going to need all the

luck we can get today, she thought.

But where was the headband? Gwen had been so busy looking down at the ground that she hadn't realised how far she had gone from where they had left Moonlight. She looked up and spun around, but couldn't see her cousin anywhere. She was now completely on her own. 'Flora?' she shouted. But her voice sounded small among the dense trees. She put her hands to her mouth and tried again. 'Flora!'

There was no answer. Gwen started back in the direction she'd come, but when she reached a towering horse chestnut tree, she stopped. She couldn't remember having seen this tree before. It had an enormous, wide trunk and twisted branches with brown and yellow leaves and white fungus growing around its raised roots. She was sure she would have remembered it. She looked round. Had she come the wrong way?

She turned back, but the further she went into the trees, the more lost Gwen became. Finally she stopped. The trees around her were bare of leaves and their branches were dry and breaking. She realised that she must be back near the Lake. She looked around, frowning. She was used to being in the forest on her own, but she usually stuck to the tracks and kept a careful eye on the direction she was travelling. Gwen knew you could work out which direction north was by seeing which side of the tree trunks the moss was growing on, but it didn't help her now because she had no idea which direction she had left Moonlight. She could have kicked herself for not checking her bearings as she had gone to look for the headband.

The shadows seemed dark in the trees around her, and Gwen began to feel a flicker of unease. A loud rustle came from the trees in front of her and she swallowed, remembering the tales she had heard of the strange beings and dangerous creatures who lived in the forest.

The rustle whispered through the trees again.

Gwen's hand instinctively reached for an arrow and she began to slowly pace backwards. The rustling got louder and Gwen's heart began to beat faster. She took a deep breath, still walking steadily back, and prepared herself to aim and fire, when suddenly she felt herself bump back

into something – *or someone. . .*

She yclped in shock and whirled round to find a familiar figure with sticking-up blond hair staring at her, his own face equally shocked.

'Arthur!' Gwen burst out.

For a moment Arthur just opened and shut his mouth like a fish. 'Gwen, you almost made me jump out of my skin! What are you doing?'

'I heard something.' Gwen glanced back round and saw a fox looking out of the bushes in front of her. So that was what had been making the rustling noise! She breathed a sigh of relief and turned back to Arthur, her earlier fear evaporating. 'What are you doing here?' she asked him.

'Just exploring, practising my archery. I like getting away from the others sometimes and coming into the forest on my own.' Arthur glanced round at the trees. 'It always feels like something exciting could happen out here – that I could have an adventure like a real knight,' he added, a hint of longing in his voice.

Gwen nodded, smiling – she knew exactly

what he meant about having adventures in the forest!

'But what about you?' Arthur continued. 'Why are you out here?'

'Uh, Flora and I came for a walk,' Gwen said quickly. 'But I've lost her.'

'How did you get separated?' Arthur asked.

'We. . . we were playing hide and seek,' Gwen invented. 'I really must find her.'

'Don't worry. I'll help you look for her,' offered Arthur. He walked over to a nearby ash tree with dry, leafless branches. 'Why don't I climb up here and see if I can spot her?'

Gwen was about to nod when she suddenly remembered Moonlight. What if Arthur looked further into the forest and saw him? How would she and Flora explain the magic white horse?

'Don't worry. I'll do it!' she said hastily.

Before Arthur could do anything, she slipped her bow off her shoulder, grabbed a branch, found a foothold and swung herself into the tree.

'Gwen!' Arthur exclaimed. 'You shouldn't be doing things like that. Let me climb up.'

Gwen grinned. 'Nope!' She scrambled further up the tree. She was used to climbing, and although her long dress made it difficult, her slim arms were strong and she was very agile. In no time at all, she was sitting on a high-up branch. She caught sight of a bright splash of red through the trees. It was Flora's poppy-red dress! Flora was standing nearby and seemed to be looking round desperately for Gwen.

'Flora!' Gwen yelled, waving, seeing her cousin's anxious face. 'Flora! I'm up here!'

Flora looked round, trying to find where the voice was coming from.

'Flora!' shouted Gwen again.

Her cousin's face finally broke into a relieved smile as she saw Gwen in the tree. 'I thought I'd lost you!' Flora shouted back. 'Stay there! I'll come over to you!' She started hurrying through the trees towards Gwen.

'I've found her!' Gwen called back down to Arthur. 'She's heading this way!' She started to climb down the tree. It was harder to go down in a dress. She held on tight to the branches, kicking her skirts away and trying to feel for footholds.

'Wait!' said Arthur. 'I'll help you.' But just as he started up the tree trunk, the branch Gwen was holding on to snapped. With a shriek, she felt herself falling through the air. Arms flailing like a windmill, she crashed down into Arthur. They both fell and hit the soft, muddy ground in a tangle of limbs.

'Ow!' they exclaimed at the same time. They looked at each other.

'You squashed me!' said Arthur.

'You squashed me more!' said Gwen. They both burst out laughing and started to sit up.

'Gwen!' Flora's shocked voice cut through the air.

Gwen and Arthur stopped laughing. Flora had come through the trees and was standing over them staring, a shocked expression on her face. 'What are you doing, Gwen? What's Arthur doing here? And what are you both doing on the floor?'

Gwen scrambled to her feet. 'Arthur was out for a walk and we bumped into each other.'

'Then Gwen fell out of the tree and bumped into me!' laughed Arthur. 'She might be brilliant at climbing up, but she's not so good at coming back down.'

Flora put her hands on her hips and looked disapproving as Gwen and Arthur got to their feet. Gwen grinned – she knew her cousin was thinking it was all very unlady-like!

'Come on then, let's all go back to the castle,' Arthur said, looking at them both. Gwen felt a moment's alarm. She and Flora couldn't go back – they had to find Lily! But how could she explain that to Arthur without telling him the truth? 'Um. . . well. . . um. . .' she stammered.

Just in time, Flora stepped forward. 'We can't come back just yet, Arthur. We have to find my headband, you see. I dropped it and we can't go back without it. You know how angry my mother would be.'

Gwen nodded, grateful for Flora's quick thinking 'Yes, we'll have to stay and look for it. You go on ahead of us, though.'

Arthur shrugged. 'Don't worry. I'll help you look for it and then we can all walk back together.'

Gwen looked at Flora. Now what were they going to do?

But Flora just smiled. 'The thing is, Arthur…' She linked arms with Gwen, 'Gwen and I have got lots of girly things to discuss on the way back.' She giggled and looked at him coyly through her eyelashes. 'We want to talk about how to braid our hair, and Gwen was just saying how she'd like to go over how best to curtsey. And then, of course, I wanted her help to choose what colour I'll have for my next dress. . . I mean, of course, you can always walk with us and listen if you want?' Flora looked at Arthur as if she really meant it.

'No, no,' Arthur said hastily, starting to back away. 'Actually, it sounds like it might be best if I leave the two of you to walk back on your own then, if you're sure you'll be all right?'

'Yes, we'll be fine,' Gwen said quickly.

'Very well. See you back at the castle!' He turned and hurried away.

Flora chuckled in satisfaction. 'That got rid of him!'

Gwen grinned at her. 'I knew there was a reason why you came with me on these adventures!' But her face fell as she realised something. 'Except now Arthur thinks I like talking about girly things like hair braiding!'

Flora's eyes glinted mischievously. 'And what does it matter what Arthur thinks?'

Gwen went a bit red. 'It doesn't. Of course it doesn't.'

'You could always borrow some of my perfume next time you see him!' Flora teased.

Gwen glared at her and changed the subject. 'I guess we'd better find your headband so we can get going again.'

'No need.' Flora reached into the pocket of her dress and pulled out the sparkling band with a flourish. 'I've already found it!'

Gwen stared at her. 'So you just said we still needed to find it so that Arthur would go away?'

Flora nodded. 'Yes.'

'It's not very lady-like to tell fibs, Flora!' Gwen teased her.

Flora gave her a cheeky look. 'I'm obviously spending far too much time with you!'

Gwen giggled and looked around. 'Right, let's find Moonlight and get going. We've got a job to do.' Excitement bubbled through her. They had another Spell Sister to rescue!

6

The Enchanted Vineyard

The girls saw a high hill rising up in front of them with a sparkling stream at the bottom of it as Moonlight galloped out of the forest and into a meadow. Silver trout were leaping out of the water and plunging in again with a splash. Near the bottom of the hill, the grass was as green as a beech leaf in spring, but further up it turned brown and dry. A sinister-looking vineyard surrounded by a tall wall was standing a little way up its slopes.

'There it is,' Gwen said to Flora. 'Fairview Vineyard.'

'I don't like the look of it,' said Flora. 'I hope we find Lily quickly so we can leave.'

Gwen nodded. 'And that Morgana doesn't send any more of her savage birds this time.' She patted the horse's neck. 'Come on, Moonlight!'

Moonlight needed no urging. He galloped towards the vineyard entrance, but as they drew closer, Gwen wrinkled her nose. The smell of rotting fruit was hanging heavily in the air. The massive gates loomed up in front of them, made of black twisted metal. They were covered with overgrown vines.

Moonlight snorted and quickly backed away.

Gwen soothed him, patting his neck. 'Steady,

boy.' He came to a halt a little way off.

Gwen and Flora dismounted and walked closer. Through the gaps in the gate they could see into the vineyard. Each vine tree was dying, its leaves turning brown, and its branches heavy with diseased bunches of grapes. The farmhouse next to the vines was deserted, the front door hanging open, and there was a windowless stone store and an abandoned pigsty nearby. There was an eerie feeling hanging in the air all around them.

Flora shuddered. 'It's horrible.'

Moonlight snorted anxiously from where he was standing. It was clear he didn't want to come any closer. He pawed the ground with a front hoof, his ears flicking as the girls got nearer to the gates. The metal they were made out of was midnight black and seemed to draw in the light. It wasn't iron. Gwen had never seen metal like it.

She reached out for the handle and then hesitated as a shiver like icy fingers suddenly trailed down her spine.

'I. . . I wish we didn't have to go in,' Flora said in a small voice.

Gwen took a breath. She felt the same, but she tried to force herself to be brave. 'I know, but we have to. We can't let Lily down!' Putting her hand on the large round handle, she turned it and pushed. With a loud creak, one of the gates swung open.

The girls stepped into the vineyard. As they did so, the gate swung shut behind them with a clang. Gwen and Flora jumped.

'How did it do that?' Flora said uneasily.

Gwen bit her lip. 'Maybe it was the wind.' Goosebumps prickled over her skin. Although there was no one in the vineyard, she felt like she should speak in a whisper. 'Where do you think Lily is trapped?' she said in a hushed voice, looking round at the mess of vines.

'I don't know,' replied Flora.

Gwen remembered what Nineve had said. 'I suppose she could be inside one of the vine trees, like Sophia was? Or she could be disguised as something else – remember, Nineve told us she could be anywhere or disguised as anything. She could even be a stone or a brick in the wall or part of the farmhouse.'

'How are we ever going to find her?' asked Flora in dismay.

'We'll just have to look hard,' Gwen said, squeezing her hand. 'Come on. The sooner we find her and release her, the sooner we can get out of here.'

They hurried towards the vines and started

searching through them. Gwen tried to ignore
the horrible sensation of rotten grapes squishing
beneath her boots and the feel of the sticky stems
of the vines as she pushed through them with her
hands.

They worked along the rows, looking at the trunks and examining any rocks or stones nearby. But they found nothing that made them think they had discovered Lily.

'I can't see any sign of her,' Gwen said, stopping and wiping her brow.

'If only we had some way of knowing where she was!' said Flora in frustration.

Gwen looked hopefully at her pendant, but it hadn't been any use when they had been trying to find Sophia, and once again it looked as it always did, revealing nothing.

Flora looked round. 'We could be here all day. Oh, where is Lily?'

Just then, a whinny rang out and Gwen looked round to see Moonlight watching them from outside the gates. He was stamping at the ground. Seeing Gwen watching him, the horse reared up on his back legs and then landed and tossed his head towards the gates.

'What's he doing?' asked Flora.

Gwen frowned. 'It's like he's trying to tell us something.' She walked towards the entrance. 'What is it, boy?'

As she got closer to the gates, the stallion whinnied again, louder and more insistent this time. He nodded his head towards the gates once more.

Gwen thought for a moment. He hadn't liked the gates from the moment they'd arrived. What was it about them that made him so jumpy? She looked at the strange black metal twisted into an intricate arrangement of swirls under the snaking, overgrown vines. She'd thought it was just a pattern, but now she realised it was like a picture – there were tendrils of metal spreading out into a familiar shape. Gwen moved closer to investigate. Vines hid part of the image, but there was something about it. . .

Gwen stopped and pulled the vines away, revealing two wide eyes, a nose, an open mouth. . . She gasped. Staring back at her in the complicated metalwork was a face. The face of a beautiful woman!

Gwen hadn't seen it before because it had been so hidden by the vines. As she looked, she could see the metal swirls spreading out from the face were strands of hair, and she could make out a woman's long, slender body too.

'What's going on, Gwen?' Flora called from behind her. 'What are you looking at?'

Gwen turned, her heart beating like a drum. 'Flora! I. . . I think I've found what we're looking for!' She touched the face. 'Lily?' she whispered.

She hardly dared hope, but then suddenly the metal started to move!

Gwen snatched her hand back as the young woman trapped in the gate began to move her mouth soundlessly, her eyes looking terrified.

'Lily, it is you!' gasped Gwen. 'Don't be scared. Nineve sent us. Flora and I are going to rescue you!' Gwen reached for the pendant. All she had to do was touch Lily with it and say the spell that Nineve had taught her, and then the sister would be free! Excitement leaped through her and she pulled the pendant over her head. This time they were going to beat Morgana easily!

But as she reached out, she saw Lily's hand. It was moving in the metal, one finger painfully and torturously straightening out and pointing down to the bottom of the gate.

'What is it— ?' Gwen began, but just then she heard Flora shriek.

'Gwen! The vines by your feet are moving! Watch out!'

Gwen felt something snaking around her ankle and looked down. Tendrils were twining around her foot! She cried out and jumped backwards but more vines shot out towards her, wrapping around her ankle and outstretched hand. Gwen felt the tendrils tighten like a noose. She couldn't get away!

'Flora!' she yelled desperately, as she was dragged back towards the strange black metal of the gate. . .

7 Attacked!

Gwen heard Flora scream in horror. She pulled back desperately, but the tendrils of the vine wrapped more and more tightly around her right wrist and ankle, their rough stems digging into her skin, hurting, gripping. . .

As Gwen struggled and tried to fight free, she saw Lily's anxious face in the metal. What would happen if the vine pulled her against the strange gates? Would she be trapped like Lily too?

'No!' she panted. She threw her weight in the other direction.

Flora came running over and reached out to try and pull Gwen free. 'Stay back!' gasped Gwen.

'No! I'm going to help you!' Grabbing hold of Gwen's arm, Flora started trying to tear the vine off. 'Let go of her!' she shouted at it.

'Be careful, Flora!' Gwen gasped. 'It'll get you too!'

Snap! As Gwen spoke, tendrils from one of the other vines by the gate shot across the ground, wrapping around both Flora's legs and arms like snakes.

Flora shrieked as the green fronds tightened around her. 'Get off me!' she cried, beating at them as best she could.

'It must be Morgana!' cried Gwen as her feet slipped over the ground. The vines were dragging her closer and closer to the gate. 'She's using Lily's magic to control these vines.'

'Wh-what are we going to do?' shouted Flora desperately.

Gwen still had one hand and leg free. The vines were stopping her getting to her bow and quiver, but she could reach her bag. Putting her free hand in, she felt cold, smooth metal touch her fingers. Of course! The iron horseshoe she'd found in the woods when she'd been looking for Flora's headband! Iron could ward off evil . . . She wasn't sure if it would work, but it was worth a try! Her fingers closed around it and she pulled it out.

Turning back, Gwen swiped at the vine's tendrils. To her relief and amazement, the second the horseshoe touched them they shrivelled and dropped away from her! Gwen fell backwards as she was abruptly released, but to her dismay, the horseshoe went shooting out of her hands as her arms flailed wildly. She crashed down to the ground and watched it skid under the gates and out of her reach. But at least she was free!

Gwen scrambled to her feet. Her wrist was sore from where the tendrils had been digging into her, but she ignored the pain. She had to help

Flora! But what could she do? If only she'd kept hold of the horseshoe she could have used it to free her cousin as well, but now it was the other side of the gates, and if she tried to get through them the vines would get her again. She looked around for another way out, but the wall was too high to climb.

Panic rushed through her as she saw the vines curl up around Flora's shoulders and waist. Gwen couldn't just stand and watch. She started forwards. 'No, don't, Gwen!' Flora cried. 'Stay back or they'll get you again!'

A tendril crept over Flora's neck and started to wind around. It began to tighten, and Gwen could see Flora had to fight for air. Fear raced through her – the vine would soon suffocate Flora. . .

'Bow and arrow!' Flora croaked.

Of course! Gwen slipped the bow from her shoulder and grabbed an arrow from her quiver. Lifting it up she pulled the string back. She took a breath to steady herself. If she got her aim wrong, she might hit Flora. She fixed her eyes on the vine that was holding Flora, aiming for its base. She breathed out and, in a movement as smooth and instinctive as blinking, she released the arrow. It flew away from her and thwacked into the base of the vine by the gate.

The tendrils jerked and but then squeezed Flora tighter, making her cry out in pain. Gwen quickly grabbed another arrow and fired again, and again, hoping that somehow one of the arrows would cut through the vine. Her fingers closed around the last arrow. As she pulled it out, she realised it was her uncle's kingfisher arrow. He would be furious if she lost it, but right now she didn't care. She looked up desperately and saw Flora still gasping in pain.

Lifting the beautiful arrow, Gwen sighted her target and let the arrow fly. The kingfisher feathers gleamed bright blue and green, a glint of goodness in the darkness of the enchanted vineyard. Her aim was true and the sharp engraved point hit the very heart of the vine. It shuddered and then fell to the ground, suddenly

lifeless. Flora staggered away, gasping as the vine's grip was released.

Slinging her bow over her shoulder, Gwen ran over to her cousin. 'Oh, Flora! You're free!' Relief overwhelmed her and she hugged Flora tight.

'You saved me!' Flora gasped.

'It was your father's kingfisher arrow,' said Gwen. 'It worked when the others didn't!'

'Kingfisher feathers,' Flora said. 'They ward off evil, remember? I bet that's why it worked!'

'Of course!' cried Gwen. 'The vines are evil because of Morgana's enchantment, so the iron and kingfisher feathers worked against them.' She looked all round. 'I hope it's only those vines by the gates that have been enchanted like that.' She didn't like to think what would happen if Morgana was controlling all the vines. She and Flora would never escape. 'We've got to free Lily and get out of here.'

'But how can we?' Flora pointed out. 'How are you going reach the gate without the vines getting you? We don't have anything left to fight them with.'

Gwen looked at the vine that had captured her. It was lying still on the ground now. But it didn't look lifeless like the other vine she had shot with the arrow. She took a cautious step towards it to see what would happen. Instantly, the tendrils stirred and the leaves rustled with a sinister sound. Gwen jumped back.

'What are we going to do?' she said anxiously. 'I can't free Lily unless I touch her with the pendant. . .'

But Gwen trailed off as she heard a faint sound building in the air – a humming, buzzing sound. Looking up into the sky she saw a dark cloud heading towards the hilltop. The strange buzzing noise was coming from it, and it was getting louder and fiercer with every second.

'What is that?' Flora said uneasily.

They watched for a few second longer and then Gwen's green eyes widened. 'I think they're hornets – thousands of them! And they're heading straight towards us!'

8

The Swarm of Hornets

'Run!' Gwen cried.

'Where to?' Flora asked, her eyes wide with panic.

'The farmhouse! It's our only hope!'

Gwen grabbed Flora's hand and, tripping and stumbling over the overgrown vines, they ran as fast as they could towards the deserted building. The hornets were swooping down on the vineyard. Glancing round, Gwen saw that these were no ordinary hornets – each yellow and black wasplike insect was as big as the palm of her hand. Their transparent wings were whirring, their eyes red and fixed on the girls. Gwen had never seen hornets so huge! Fear pounded through her, but the farmhouse was close, the door hanging open. If they could just reach it.

An evil laugh rang out suddenly and the buzzing faded slightly. Gwen looked round again and gave a startled cry. The hornets had stopped in the sky and were moving into a shape as if controlled by something – or someone. 'Look, Flora!' Gwen whispered, gripping her cousin's hand tighter.

The hornets had formed into the image of a woman's face. She had dark eyes and long dark straight hair.

'You shall not free Lily!' Her mouth moved and her voice buzzed out. 'I am Morgana Le Fay, and I will not be defeated by two mortal girls. My powers are too strong. Leave this place at once!'

Gwen could feel Flora trembling but although she felt scared too, she wasn't going to give up. 'No!' she said bravely. 'We said we'd

rescue Lily and we will!'

'Silence, child!' shrieked Morgana through the hornets. 'You dare to challenge Morgana Le Fay? You will suffer for this! If you will not leave, then prepare to face my hornets!' With a furious scream, her face vanished. The hornets immediately clumped together and flew at the girls.

Gwen and Flora only just had time to reach the farmhouse. Flora's cloak fell off, but they didn't stop. They flung themselves into the building and Gwen slammed the door behind them. A shower of dust fell from the farmhouse beams. The large room they were in was empty, with just stone walls, a bare fireplace and a stone floor. Outside, the sound of the hornets bombarding the stone walls, door, and narrow diamond-paned windows was terrifying.

'What if the windows break?' Flora panted anxiously.

Gwen swallowed. She didn't want to think about that. She had no arrows left, nothing in her travelling bag, and the house was empty. She paced up and down as the hornets thudded against the glass like hailstones in a storm.

'Think, think,' she muttered to herself. 'What do you know about hornets?' She stopped by a window. 'Light! I remember Aunt Matilda once telling me how to get rid of hornets – they're attracted by light, so when it's dark you can light a candle and trap them.'

'But we haven't got any candles, and it isn't dark,' said Flora. 'We'll need to think of something else.'

Gwen went to the window, her thoughts racing. 'What about the rotting grapes? Don't hornets like sticky things like that? Maybe I could run out and see if I can use the grapes to distract them?'

'No, no, that won't work,' Flora told her. 'It's wasps who like sticky sweet things, not hornets. Hornets like meat. But we haven't got any of that either.' She rubbed her forehead. 'I know there's something else about them, I just can't remember . . .'

Gwen watched the hornets outside. Lots of them were swarming round Flora's cloak, swooping down on it viciously. 'That's strange.' Gwen said. 'They seem to be aiming at your cloak. Maybe it's the colour? Perhaps they don't like red or something?'

'No!' Flora gasped. 'It's not that! I bet it's my perfume, Gwen! They can smell it on the cloak. That's what I was trying to remember! Hornets are driven crazy by perfume. Mother told me it's very dangerous to go anywhere near a hornet's nest with perfume on because it sends them into a frenzy.'

Gwen felt an idea start to form in her brain. She glanced out of the window, her gaze falling on the stone hut. 'So, if we could empty your perfume out somewhere, the hornets might follow the smell?' she said thoughtfully.

'Yes. I suppose so,' Flora said cautiously. 'But that would mean one of us going out there. . .'

'I can do it!' declared Gwen bravely. She pulled off her own cloak. 'I'll soak this in the perfume and throw it into the hut over there. If we're right, the hornets will follow the smell and I'll shut the door on them. Then they'll be trapped!'

'And if it doesn't work?' faltered Flora.

Gwen took a breath. 'It has to.' She marched forward and took the perfume bottle from Flora before her cousin could stop her.

'No, Gwen! It's too dangerous! You could get stung!' Flora protested, but Gwen was already pulling out the cork stopper and tipping some of the perfume over her cloak. The pungent smell filled the room.

'Here goes!' Gwen strode to the door. Her breath was short in her throat and she could feel her hands sweating, but she knew she had to do something. If she and Flora just stayed in the farmhouse, they'd be trapped by the hornets and Morgana would have succeeded. She put her hand on the door handle. She really hoped her plan was going to work.

'Gwen!' Flora stepped forward but it was too late. Gwen had pulled open the door and dashed out!

The sound of enraged buzzing filled her ears. She sprinted across the ground towards the stone storeroom, letting more perfume trail out behind her. She didn't think she'd ever run so fast in her life. She could hear the hornets chasing her, feel them as they hit against her body, but in a flash, she had reached the door of the hut.

Bundling up the cloak, she threw it in through the open door and crouched down. For a terrifying moment the world seemed to stand still. She braced herself for the hornets' stings – but Flora had been right. The smell of the perfume was all the hornets could think about. They shot in through the open doorway and swarmed towards the cloak, stinging it furiously. As the last few swooped in, Gwen slammed the door shut and pulled the stiff metal bolt across. There were no windows and no gaps in the roof. The stone walls of the hut were strong. She and Flora were safe!

Her spirits lifting, Gwen raced back to the house. Flora had been watching anxiously from the window. She flung the door open and ran out to meet Gwen. 'You did it!' Flora cried and they swung each other round.

'We've got rid of the hornets!' cried Gwen. 'Come on! Let's go and rescue Lily!'

'But how?' cried Flora as they ran towards the black metal gates. 'The vine's still there!'

'I'll just have to be quick,' Gwen said, pulling the pendant over her head. 'If I free Lily fast enough then maybe the vine won't have a chance to get hold of me. We really can't stay here any longer! There's no telling what might happen if Morgana realises what's happened with her hornets!'

Reaching the gates, Gwen dashed forward towards the metal figure of Lily. Instantly, the enchanted vine snapped out, curling round her ankles and wrists, but she ignored it. Pressing the blue pendant against Lily's image in the curled metal gate, Gwen gasped out the spell Nineve had taught her:

*'Spell Sister of Avalon, I now release
Return to the island and help bring peace!'*

The vines were biting into her skin but Gwen hardly noticed. She watched, open-mouthed, as the gates started to creak and shudder. The

tendrils of metal that formed the image of Lily
began to shiver and tremble, and Gwen saw the
sister of Avalon's arms and legs start to move,
like the metal itself was animated. Then, before

Gwen and Flora's very eyes, Lily stepped right out of the gate!

As she stood before them, Lily turned from the elaborate swirls of metal into a beautiful woman. Her long black hair flowed down to her feet, and her green eyes were alight in her pale face. Her dress was the colour of spring grass and she had a headband made from delicate silver leaves in her hair. 'I'm free!' she cried.

Gwen whooped, but as she did so, she felt the vines tighten further. They began yanking her furiously back towards the black metal gates!

'Help!' she cried, but then she lost her balance and fell forward, her hands reaching out towards the gate where Lily had been imprisoned.

9

Lily's Magic

Gwen heard Flora cry out in alarm, and she thought she was doomed – but then a lilting voice cut through the air:

'Plants of the kingdom, blossom and bloom
Return from the depths of Morgana's gloom.'

The tendrils that were pulling Gwen instantly

stopped and loosened their grip. Gwen felt the vines instead begin to gently lift her into the air and set her back on her feet, turning green and vivid as they did so. She gasped and then turned to look around her. All over the vineyard everything was changing. The dying and diseased vines were becoming healthy again, their branches lifting up, their leaves and stems tumbling over each other, with bunches of perfectly round, ripe grapes now hanging heavily from the branches.

'Everything's changing!' Flora said, running over.

'My magic is working.'

Flora and Gwen turned to the beautiful sister of Avalon. She was smiling broadly. 'I have my powers back!' Her eyes, the colour of the new vine leaves, sparkled. 'And now Morgana won't be able to kill the plants or make them evil!' She swirled round, her arms out. 'Oh, it's so wonderful to be free!'

'So this means the vineyard will be all right again?' Gwen said. 'Uncle Richard won't be getting any more sour wine?'

'Yes!' Lily answered with a smile. 'I'm sure your uncle will be much happier with his wine now!'

Flora squeezed Gwen's hand. 'That was amazing! I can't believe the way you ran out to the shed with those hornets chasing you and freed Lily even though the vines got hold of you!'

'Yes,' agreed Lily. 'I thank you from the bottom of my heart for freeing me, Guinevere.'

Gwen blushed. 'Flora, was brilliant too! She was the one who remembered that hornets hate perfume.' She smiled at her cousin. 'If you hadn't been here, I'd probably have still been trapped in the farmhouse! I'll never tease you about knowing about household stuff again.'

'What? Never!' said Flora, raising her eyebrows disbelievingly.

Gwen grinned. 'Well, maybe only sometimes!'

'I cannot thank you both enough,' Lily said warmly. 'And now I think I have something that is yours.'

She clicked her fingers and called out a word, her voice sounding like the rustle of leaves in the spring breeze. The green vine near the broken gate reared up and reached towards Gwen. She took a step back in alarm for a moment, but then one of the vines' leaves opened and she realised it was holding out her uncle's special kingfisher arrow.

'Now the vine is released from Morgana's evil enchantment, the kingfisher feather no longer hurts it,' Lily explained with a smile. 'Take it, Guinevere. Kingfisher feathers are precious and must be treasured.'

'And this one's not even mine,' said Gwen, feeling relieved she wouldn't have to explain its loss to her uncle. 'Thank you,' she said to the vine as she took the arrow. The vine's leaves rustled and it sank back down.

'We should go back to the Lake,' Flora said as Gwen slipped the arrow into her quiver. She turned to Lily. 'Your sister, Sophia, is already waiting on Avalon.'

Lily's face lit up. 'But that is wonderful news! So Sophia is safe?'

Flora nodded happily.

'And my other sisters?' Lily asked.

'I'm afraid they're still trapped,' answered Gwen. 'But we're going to save them. We have to free all of them so that they can return to Avalon and restore its magic before the next lunar eclipse! We can't let Morgana Le Fay succeed.'

Lily smiled. 'I can see the pendant was right to choose you.' She sighed. 'But how shall we get to Avalon? I can use my magic to transport myself there, but I'm not sure I will be able to take you both as well...'

'You don't need to worry about us. We've got our own way of travelling.' Gwen grinned. Lifting her fingers to her mouth, she whistled shrilly.

There was a whinny and then Moonlight came galloping towards the entrance to the vineyard. He leaped through the hole in the broken gate and stopped beside them, his white mane cascading down his neck.

Gwen stroked him. 'This is Moonlight. He'll carry us back.' She scrambled on to his back and helped Flora up behind her. 'We'll see you by the Lake, Lily!'

The sister laughed. 'May Moonlight carry you safely back. I will see you there. Farewell!' She clapped her hands and a silver mist swirled around her, hiding her from view. When it cleared, the girls saw Lily had vanished.

Flora wrapped her arms round Gwen's waist. 'Let's go!'

'Come on, Moonlight!' Gwen cried. She touched her heels to the horse's sides. He plunged forward and began to speed away, leaving the now-green and fertile vineyard behind. Moonlight galloped down the hill, as sure-footed as a mountain goat. They soared past the sparkling stream at the bottom and raced into the forest. Gwen laughed in delight as the trees whizzed by. She felt like she could go on riding Moonlight forever, but all too soon they reached the Lake.

Nineve and Lily were standing there talking,

their hands clasped together. They looked round as Moonlight whinnied and came to a stop, and Gwen and Flora dismounted.

'Oh,' Flora said, looking disappointed. 'I thought all the plants around the Lake would look green and healthy again.' She glanced around. All the shrubs and bushes were just as brown and dry as it had been earlier that day. 'Can't you work your magic here, Lily?' she asked.

'I'm afraid not,' sighed Lily. 'I can repair the damage done by Morgana while she was misusing my power, but the forest around here is slowly dying because Avalon's magic is fading. My magic is too weak on its own to change that. Only when all eight Spell Sisters come together on the island again will the magic return here and the kingdom be saved from ruin.'

'The other six sisters must be released, and

soon,' Nineve added.

Gwen nodded. 'Don't worry, we can do it.'

'We'll do whatever it takes,' Flora agreed.

'I will continue to use my magic to try and track them down,' Nineve said. 'But you may well face Morgana again. Girls, I cannot thank you enough. You are so brave.' The Lady of the Lake smiled at them both. 'For now, Lily is keen to return to Avalon and help Sophia protect the little magic that is left there. Come!' She clapped her hands. A sparkling mist surrounded the girls and they suddenly found themselves floating up into the air and then coming to a rest on the surface of the glassy Lake.

Gwen knew she should be used to the sensation, but it still felt as magical as the first time it had happened. It was amazing to be able to walk across the water. Nineve whispered a word and the purple mist parted and the island came into view. Nineve led the way through the mist with the girls and Lily following closely.

Nineve waited in the water while Lily and the girls stepped out on to Avalon. They walked up the path that led through the orchard of apple trees up to the only house on the island. Avalon was still barren and the air was silent – the only movement the trail of smoke coming from the chimney of the house. However, Gwen's sharp eyes saw that here and there, there were flashes of green – a few blades of grass, buds forming on the apple trees' bare branches, the tips of new plants pushing out of the soil. Gwen smiled – it gave her hope that they would succeed in their task.

She didn't have time to investigate closely, though. Lily was already running up the path, and as she reached the door, it was flung open.

Sophia stood there, her bright red hair cascading around her shoulders, her eyes shining. 'Lily!' she exclaimed in delight.

The two sisters embraced.

'Guinevere and Flora freed me!' exclaimed Lily. Sophia beamed at the girls.

'Thank you! Please, come inside,' she said, holding open the door. The girls could see a merry fire burning in the grate and food on the table. 'Sit down.'

'We'd better not,' said Gwen reluctantly. She wished they could go in and talk to the sisters – that would be amazing – but she was aware the afternoon light was fading. 'It's getting late and everyone at the castle will start wondering where we are if we don't get back in time for supper.'

Flora nodded. 'If we're not back soon they'll start looking for us.'

'We'll come again though,' said Gwen with a grin, 'when we free another of your sisters!'

'Wait! Before you go,' said Lily, 'let me give you something to say thank you for rescuing me.' She looked at Gwen's necklace with the blue pendant and the stone of fire agate that Sophia had given to her. 'I shall give you another gift that will help you if you succeed in your quest to free our sisters, just as Sophia did.'

Lily ran out of the house and picked one of the new green blades of grass that was growing beside the path. Then she waved her right hand over it and cupped her palms together. Lifting her hands to her lips she whispered a word, then slowly lowered her hands and opened them. The girls gasped as they saw that the single blade of grass had now turned into a glowing green gemstone.

'It is an emerald,' Lily said softly. 'Keep it safe, you will need it one day.'

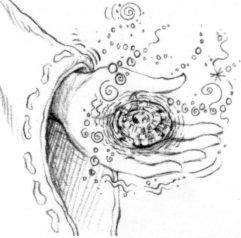

She touched the emerald to Gwen's necklace. There was a silver flash and the beautiful stone attached itself to the necklace.

Gwen touched it. 'Thank you!' she breathed.

Lily smiled. 'Farewell.'

Gwen and Flora hugged the two sisters and then ran back down to the water's edge, where the Lady of the Lake was waiting. Lily and Sophia waved from the house doorway as the girls followed Nineve back through mist and across the Lake to the forest.

10

Back to the Castle

'You have done so well,' Nineve said as the girls stepped on to dry land. 'You have freed two Spell Sisters, but there are six remaining who must still be released.' Nineve started to sink into the Lake. 'Listen for my call. And until then, may the magic of Avalon watch over you.'

She disappeared into the water. Suddenly everywhere seemed very still and quiet. The silence was broken by Moonlight coming over to the girls, his hoofs clopping softly on the rocks by the Lake shore.

Gwen breathed out and patted him. 'Will you take us back to the castle, boy?'

Moonlight nodded.

Gwen vaulted on to Moonlight's back and helped Flora up behind her. 'Another adventure over,' she said.

'But more still to come,' said Flora. 'I just hope we don't meet any more evil vines or giant hornets next time.'

'Hmmm,' Gwen replied. 'I think I know something even angrier than a swarm of giant hornets.'

'What?' said Flora in alarm.

Gwen grinned. 'Your father, if he realises his arrow is missing! We'd better get it back to the castle as quickly as possible. Hang on tight!' She touched her heels to Moonlight's sides as Flora grabbed her around the waist. With an eager whinny, the white stallion plunged forward. They galloped into the trees.

Moonlight took them all the way to the forest edge, and then Gwen and Flora dismounted and gave him a pat. 'We'll see you when it's time for our next adventure,' Gwen said, giving him a hug.

Moonlight nuzzled her and Flora and then turned away, slipping back through the trees and into the shadows.

Gwen checked the sun. It was streaking the sky golden and pink as it set behind the castle. 'We'd better hurry,' she said to Flora. Supper time was always at six o'clock.

'I hope no one's noticed we were gone for so long,' said Flora.

They ran as fast as they could up the hill to the castle. Both of them were tired after the long day, but they didn't stop until they were over the drawbridge and inside. The ground floor had a storeroom with doors that led into the enormous kitchens. Luckily there was no one in there to see the girls arrive, but they could hear the sound of voices and feet upstairs in the Great Hall as the household gathered. They could smell the stew being prepared in the kitchens amidst the clattering of pans and plates.

'Come on!' urged Gwen, setting off up the stairs.

'Wait!' called Flora. 'We're all dirty and still in our travelling clothes. And you still have your bow and quiver! People are bound to ask where we've been if they see us like this.'

Gwen nodded and hurried back down. She

hid her bow and arrows behind some sacks of flour – she'd come back for them later. Then she and Flora found a small butt of water and quickly wiped their faces. 'Our dresses will cover our outdoor boots,' Gwen said. 'Let's do our hair.'

Flora found a comb in her pocket and they quickly smoothed down their hair and brushed the mud off their dresses.

'Now we just have to sneak in without anyone noticing us,' said Gwen. 'It'll be easier if we go in one at a time. You go into the hall first. I'll go and put your father's arrow back in the upstairs chambers and then join you down there. We'll pretend we've been back for ages.'

They ran up the stairs together and Flora went to the big door. 'Good luck,' she mouthed, as she opened it and slipped quietly inside.

Gwen ran on up the next flight of stairs,

hiding the arrow in her skirts. She knocked cautiously on the wooden door to the chamber, but there was no reply. She went in and, to her relief, the arrows were still there on the tabletop. Gwen hurried over and pulled the kingfisher arrow out, putting it back with the others. She sighed in relief.

'What are you doing?' A boy's voice came from behind her.

Gwen jumped in the air and swung round.

Arthur was standing in the doorway to the chamber, looking at her curiously.

'I. . . um. . . I. . .' She could feel her cheeks going red.

Arthur smiled. 'It's all right. I know.'

'You do?' Gwen stared at him in shock.

He nodded. 'You just wanted to have a look at Sir Richard's new arrows, didn't you? I thought I'd sneak a peek before supper too.'

'Yes.' Gwen recovered herself and nodded quickly. 'Yes, that's right. You caught me!'

Arthur grinned. 'Sir Richard wanted someone to fetch him a quill from up here, so I thought I'd grab the opportunity to come and take a look.' He joined her at the table. 'When I'm a knight, I'll have arrows just like these!' he declared. 'They are arrows that are perfect for having amazing adventures.'

Gwen hid a smile. 'Yes,' she said. 'They are.'

Arthur glanced at her. 'Gwen, you're not like other girls, are you? You're so good at archery, and climbing – well, not so good at climbing down, perhaps!' They both laughed, remembering what had happened in the forest earlier. 'Don't you wish you were a boy and could become a knight when you get older?'

Gwen thought about her day. If only Arthur knew what she and Flora had really been doing out in the forest! She wished she could tell him, but she just shook her head. 'No,' she said. 'I like being me.' She ran to the door. 'Race you to supper, Arthur!'

Arthur leaped after her and, laughing together, they charged down the stairs to the Great Hall.

In a Forest Clearing

In the heart of the forest, Morgana Le Fay heard her raven crying out in surprise. She stalked out of a hollowed-out trunk of an enormous oak tree and stopped dead.

'No,' she hissed out, staring around her. Only a few hours ago the nearby trees had been blackened and twisted, but now their branches were now covered with bright red and gold leaves.

Everywhere she looked was a riot of autumnal colour - glossy conkers popping out of green shells, red rosehips hanging on the branches, juicy blackberries weighing down the stems of the bramble bushes. The sorceress's voice rose. 'No! Those girls can't have freed Lily! They can't! How can my hornets and enchanted vines have failed me? It is not possible.'

But as if to prove it, a red-and-yellow leaf detached itself from one of the branches high above and fluttered down to the ground in front of her feet.

Morgana screamed a curse. A squirrel darted up a nearby tree trunk swishing its tail. With an enraged cry, Morgana flicked a lightning bolt out of her fingers straight at him. He chattered in alarm and leaped for the safety of the higher branches just in time.

'This cannot continue,' Morgana hissed, starting to pace up and down, her jet-black eyes full of rage. 'Those girls must not be allowed to free any more of the sisters of Avalon. I will stop them – whatever it takes!'

The raven shrieked and flew down on to her shoulder. Morgana touched his feathers and, scowling blackly, she swept back into her lair inside the oak trunk.

Behind her, the autumn leaves trembled.

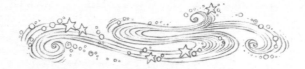

Read on for a sneak peek of the
next SPELL SISTERS adventure!

Gwen grasped the pendant with trembling fingers and held it up to see properly. A mist was swirling over its blue surface. As the mist cleared, the beautiful face of Nineve, the Lady of the Lake, was revealed in the depths of the stone.

'Guinevere,' Nineve whispered, seeming to look straight from the pendant deep into Gwen's eyes.

Gwen felt excitement surge through her. Her

fingers tightened on the pendant. 'Yes, Nineve! Do you need us? Have you found another Spell Sister?'

'I have.' Nineve's voice was soft and musical. 'I have seen where Isabella, the Spell Sister with the power over all insects, is trapped. Come to the Lake and I will show you what my magic has revealed.'

Gwen glanced at Flora, who was peering over her shoulder. What were they going to do? How *could* they go? They were miles from the Lake.

'Will you come now, my friends?' urged Nineve.

'Oh, Nineve,' Gwen said. 'We're not at Halston Castle, we're at another house quite far away. Even if we could get to the Lake, we wouldn't be back until very late, and there's a big celebration here tonight that we have to go to.'

'Oh dear, what unfortunate timing! I fear Isabella may be in grave danger and really needs your help. . .' said Nineve.

Gwen felt awful. How could she go to a party when one of the Spell Sisters needed her? She made up her mind. She couldn't. 'All right! We'll come!' she declared.

'Gwen, how can we do that?' said Flora, looking at her friend with concern.

Gwen stood her ground. 'We'll see you soon, Nineve.'

'I will be waiting,' said Nineve, smiling. 'Thank you so much, girls!' The mist swirled across the pendant again and her image vanished.

Gwen turned to Flora, who was staring at her as if she was mad.

'Why did you tell Nineve we'd go? We

can't. How would we get there and back in time?' Flora said.

'We have to try,' replied Gwen. 'Isabella needs us. Don't you want to help?'

'Of *course* I do.' Flora seemed to be wavering the more she thought about it. 'It would be wonderful to have another adventure, and I really want to help. It's just the party is tonight, and everyone will be so worried if we're not here. It will ruin Bethany's birthday. We can't do that.'

Gwen bit her lip. She might not like Bethany much, but she didn't want to spoil her celebration, or make people worry about them. What could they do? *Oh, if only we could get to the Lake quickly and find out where Isabella is, but still be back in time to play our instruments,* she thought, *but how can we possibly do that?*

A picture of a pure white horse filled her mind. 'If only we had Moonlight with us here!' she cried.

Moonlight was a wild stallion that Gwen and Flora had found in the forest during their first adventure. Gwen had fed him an apple from Avalon which had tamed him and given him the power to gallop incredibly fast. It also meant he could understand where the girls needed to go and what they wanted him to do. If only he was nearby, they would be able to race to the Lake and back in no time at all. Gwen's fingers closed around the pendant again. *Oh, Moonlight,* she thought desperately, *I really wish you were here!*

A sharp tingle jumped through her hands. Gwen dropped the pendant in surprise.

'What's the matter?' said Flora, noticing Gwen's startled expression.

'I. . . I felt something strange,' Gwen stammered. 'It was like a shock or something ran through my fingers from the pendant. I was just thinking about Moonlight, wishing he was here, and. . . ' Gwen broke off as a faint whinny rang through the air.

'What was that?' said Flora.

Gwen caught her breath. Surely it couldn't be Moonlight, could it?

The girls heard the sound of galloping hooves getting closer and closer. A few seconds later, a white stallion came soaring over the wall of the manor house garden. He raced across the grass towards them.

'It's Moonlight!' cried Gwen in astonishment. 'He must have got here by magic!'

Flora gaped, her mouth opening and shutting like one of the golden carp in the fishpond. 'B-but what if someone sees him!' she stammered. 'Gwen! We'll be in so much trouble! He can't be here. He just can't!'

'Well, he is!' Gwen laughed.

Moonlight stopped and shook back his long mane. Throwing her arms round his neck, Gwen cried: 'Oh, Moonlight, it's so good to see you!'

The horse neighed softly and nuzzled her shoulder.

'Gwen!' Flora exclaimed, looking around frantically. 'One of the servants could come out at any moment. Or Mother might come looking for us.'

'Then let's get out of here!' said Gwen. 'Will you take us to the Lake, Moonlight?'

Moonlight whinnied and stamped a front hoof.

Gwen chuckled. 'I think that means yes!' Taking hold of Moonlight's mane, she hitched up her skirts and vaulted on to his back. She was very athletic and an experienced rider, although the ponies she normally rode at the castle were nothing like the beautiful stallion. But Gwen was getting used to riding him now. 'Let's go, Flora!'

She saw Flora hesitate. 'It will be all right, I promise!' Gwen urged. 'We'll be back as soon as we can. You know how fast Moonlight can gallop.' She looked pleadingly at her cousin. 'Please, Flora. Avalon's depending on us!'

Flora pushed her flute into the pocket of her dress. 'Very well,' she said with a smile. 'But what about your harp, Gwen?'

'It'll have to stay here. I can't take it with me,' said Gwen.

'We should hide it, just in case Mother does

come out.' Flora tucked it down behind the bench in the long grass. 'We can always say we moved on somewhere else to practise.' Then, taking hold of Gwen's hand, Flora scrambled behind her on to Moonlight's back.

Gwen waited until Flora was settled and then clapped her heels to Moonlight's sides. With a joyful whinny, the stallion set off. He cantered straight towards the garden wall.

'H-he's going awfully fast,' Flora said nervously.

'He's got to get up some speed so we can jump!' Gwen called.

'Jump? Can't we go through the gates? Gwen, I've never jumped before!' Flora squealed as the red bricks loomed in front of them.

'Just hang on tight!' shouted Gwen. The wall came closer. Gwen felt Moonlight gather himself. As he leaped upwards, Flora shrieked and shut her eyes, but Gwen whooped in delight. It was like flying!

The stallion landed safely on the other side.

'Oh my goodness! Oh my goodness!' gasped Flora, gripping Gwen's waist. 'I feel sick!'

'Go, Moonlight!' Gwen cried to the horse.

Will Gwen and Flora be able to rescue Isabella?

Read the rest of

ISABELLA
THE BUTTERFLY SISTER

to find out!

MAKE A BEAUTIFUL BOUQUET OF PAPER LILIES!

Lily's magic controls the power of plants, but you don't need magic to make a lovely bouquet of paper lilies! Just follow these simple instructions and watch your blooms come to life. . .

What you'll need:

+ Different coloured paper (thicker paper works best, but any kind will do)
+ Green and yellow craft pipe cleaners
+ Sticky tape
+ Scissors
+ A pencil
+ Ribbon (optional)

Remember to always be careful when you're working with scissors or ask a grown-up to help you.

HOW TO MAKE YOUR FLOWERS

1. Trace an outline of your hand on to the paper with your pencil and cut out the shape. One hand-shape will make one flower, so cut out as many as you want for your bouquet.

2. Roll each finger of the hand-shape round your pencil to form curls. These will be the petals of your lily.

3. Now roll the handprint vertically so the thumb
and little finger meet and the hand forms
a funnel shape. Secure the side with sticky tape.

4. Cut a yellow pipe cleaner into a short piece – around
eight centimetres – and shape it into a 'U'. Curl the
ends of the pipe cleaner slightly, so that it's not sharp
at the top. This will form the stamen of your lily.

5. Wrap the top of a green pipe cleaner round the
bottom of the yellow 'U' you've just created and then
insert the green stem into the centre of your paper lily.
Pull the green pipe cleaner through until the yellow
'U' sits nicely in the middle of the flower.

6. Repeat the steps above to make several lilies,
then gather your flowers together, wrap another pipe
cleaner or some ribbon around the stems and voilá,
you have a bunch of beautiful paper lilies!

TOP TIPS

+ *Lilies come in lots of colours, so
you can create a really bright bunch of
flowers by using different coloured paper.*

+ *If you can't find any pipe cleaners,
you can use a green drinking straw
for the flower stem and paper for
the yellow stamen.*

Place your bouquet
in a vase to brighten up your
room, or give it to someone
else to cheer up
their day!

VISIT WWW.SPELLSISTERS.CO.UK AND

Plus lots of other enchanted extras!

Spell Sisters news

Explore Avalon

More about Gwen and Flora's quest

Spell Sister profiles

Activity sheets

Wallpapers

Your chance to get in touch with us

ENTER THE MAGICAL WORLD OF AVALON!